Beans and Lolo's
BIG
Bike Ride

Written by
R. J. Kinderman

Illustrated by
Mary Waterfall

To Nora Sara Carlos

follow your dreams

SPINNING WHEELS PUBLISHING

Publisher's Cataloging-in-Publication
(Provided by Quality Books, Inc.)

Kinderman, R. J.
    Beans and Lolo's big bike ride / written by R. J. Kinderman ; illustrated by Mary Waterfall.
      pages cm
    SUMMARY: In this rhyming story, two children bike around the United States. Along the way, they visit many national landmarks and experience the rich geography, landscape and diversity of America. Audience: Grades K-3.
      ISBN: 978-0-9856469-1-2
    1. Bicycle touring--United States--Juvenile fiction. 2. United States--Description and travel—Juvenile fiction. 3. Stories in rhyme. [1. Bicycle touring--Fiction. 2. United States--Description and travel--Fiction. 3. Stories in rhyme.] I. Waterfall, Mary, illustrator. II. Title.

PZ8.3.K5655Bea 2015   [E]
                                                           QBI15-600044

Interior and cover/dust jacket layout by Heather McElwain, Turtle Bay Creative

Very special thanks to the teacher focus group at Spooner Elementary School in Spooner, Wisconsin, and the teacher focus group at Merrill Elementary School in Oshkosh, Wisconsin, for their contribution in evaluating and critiquing Beans and Lolo's Big Bike Ride for use in the elementary classroom.

Thank you also to Sarah Darwin, Educational Consultant and Director of Instruction, for evaluating and aligning Beans and Lolo's Big Bike Ride with curriculum standards for grade levels K–3.

Thank you also to Heather McElwain of Turtle Bay Creative, who with creative skills and endless patience helped this author turn dreams into reality.   —RJK

To our son Ben (Beans), his wife Lauren (Lolo),
and our beautiful grandchildren, Hattie and Calvin,
wishing them a life filled
with happiness and adventure.
—RJK ("Bumpa")

To my husband Gene, for his
support and patience during
endless hours of art projects.
—Mary Waterfall

Friends Beans and Lolo
no longer ride trikes.
They now ride two-wheeled
boy and girl bikes.

With their helmets on safely, and lunch packed away,
the two friends set off to cross the big USA.

California

They passed brown buffalo
and white woolly sheep.

They crossed **wide** sunny prairies of gold **waving wheat**.

Under twinkling stars

Hop-Along fell asleep.

A mountain with faces and eagles that soar

South Dakota's Mt. Rushmore

looked down on two friends
riding past Mt. Rushmore.

Past ten thousand lakes,
Beans and Lolo did weave,
through forests of trees
on a **blustery breeze.**

Beans and Lolo were **tired.** Their bikes became **tippy.**
They had to **take care** across the big **Mississippi.**

They biked past red barns and cows black and white.

They rolled through tall corn. Oh my! What a sight!

They passed **Superior** and **Michigan, Huron** and **Erie.**
After Lake **Ontario** . . .
even **Hop-Along** was weary.

They found a new ocean as they biked to the east,
with creepy red creatures that were quite scary beasts.

Far out in the harbor,
a lady stood tall
for liberty, freedom,
and a good life for all.

Americans all love their country, it's true—
their Capitol and flag, proud red, white, and blue.

U.S. Capitol
Washington D.C.

As the hills reached the **clouds**,
Beans and Lolo grew pokey.
They had to be strong
climbing **mountains** named **Smoky**.

NORTH CAROLINA

GREAT SMOKY
MOUNTAINS
NATIONAL PARK

They pedaled and pedaled
till very much later.
There, crossing the road
was a **big-toothed, green gator.**

Florida

Now heading for home, they shouted "Hurrah,"
with beads on their bike from merry Mardi Gras.

A flag with one star flies so proudly we know,
thanks to all who stood tall at Fort Alamo.

They both rolled to a stop and sat down in the sand,
not believing their eyes at a canyon so **grand**.

They spied **snakes** and **lizards** and **armadillos**, oh my!
And the long arms of **cactus** touched the hot desert sky.

NEVADA

Welcome Home Beans, Lolo & Hop-Along

Pacific Ocean

Now back where they'd started
with no road left to roam,

they were happy to be back
to their home sweet home.

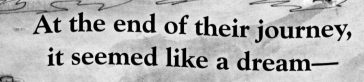

At the end of their journey,
it seemed like a dream—

all the people they'd met
and the places they'd seen.

Beans and Lolo were home.
Their big bike ride was done.

It was time to start dreaming about the next one.